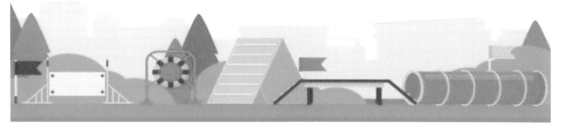

CW00742674

Copyright 2020 'The Adventures of Eddie Lightning' by Jane Norman

DEDICATIONS

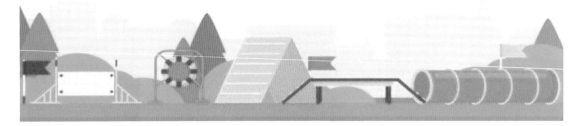

I would like to dedicate this book to all of Eddie Lightning's social media followers, who are a constant encouragement in the writing of his blogs and books. The 'woofderful' comments we receive every day are my inspiration for writing.

I would also like to dedicate this book to Eddie Lightning's agility and hoopers teachers for their patience and forgiveness each week and to my loving, supportive family. Without all your support, these books would not have been written.

INTRODUCTION

Once upon a time there was a superhero doggy called Eddie Lightning who loved to do agility. He went to agility lessons at a Dog Training Centre close to his home.

Eddie Lightning met some pawsome friends whilst there. His friends' names were Bobby, Lola, Isla and Skye. Eddie Lightning turned the sessions into a series of antics, whenever he could!

The agility sessions were once a week in a very big open field. On Eddie Lightning's arrival, he would begin by roaming around the whole field in search of any treats that might have been dropped during other training sessions.

As Eddie Lightning lived for treats, he knew that there would be some random treats he could sniff out and grab before the session began.

INTRODUCTION

He would also combine that search with saying hello to other fellow doggies, who had arrived for the session.

Everypawdy called him either Eddie, Eddie L, Lightning or Eddie Lightning.

These other doggies were sitting and waiting patiently, unlike Eddie Lightning, who didn't do patience.

He, nor anypawdy else, would know how each session would be. It all depended on how much super power charge he had left in him at the time.

It would also depend on what mood Eddie Lightning was in, as to whether he felt he would do the honour of being a good doggy or a mischievous doggy. Some part of most lessons ended in mischief.

LESSON 1 ESCAPADES

Eddie Lightning joined the beginner's agility class and got lots of fuss from the trainers.

"Wowza my first lesson was pawtastic. I took to it like a duck takes to water", said Eddie Lightning.

Eddie Lightning learnt how to jump over big colourful jumps and also learnt how to wait for his mummy to tell him when to start running, well most of the time. "Now, that was a bit of a difficult task, as I am mummy's shadow and where she goes, I go" he said.

The trainer had to sit on the, sometimes, cold and damp floor, holding Eddie Lightning and bribing him with treats, if he wouldn't sit still.

This took a number of attempts to get right. He kept running before he was told to and the trainer had to bring him back.

Eddie Lightning thought the more he did it wrong, the more treats he would get and he wasn't wrong BOL.

"Mummy had to get to the correct position to begin, then the trainer would let me follow", said Eddie Lightning.

"Mummy would run at the side of me holding a treat or my ball to encourage me to jump and to follow in the right direction."

"My biggest training issue was sitting and staying until I was called to move, no surprise there BOL", he said in a cheeky voice.

"All in all, it was a good session and I did well, if I don't mind saying so myself", said Eddie Lightning.

Mummy said, "I think it was just beginner's luck, which won't last".

I replied, "Mummy, you need to have more confidence in my 'behaviour' super powers! Where's the trust?"

LESSON 2 ANTICS

"Oh my doglets, what an entertaining evening at agility I had this time! I, of course, did everything 'my way', which made everypawdy laugh", said Eddie Lightning.

"We had to go up, across and down ramps, which is called the 'dog walk'. At the end, we had to do touch contact, which is two paws off the ramp and two paws on the ramp, touching an object with our nose, before being rewarded with a treat", he explained in an excited tone.

"Mummy and the trainer were very impressed with me, as I did it right first time" said Eddie Lightning wagging his tail.

He loved doing the ramp; he felt his super powers kick in to help him to stay upright.

"I wanted to spend the rest of the lesson doing the ramp, but the trainers had other ideas", moaned Eddie Lightning.

Eddie Lightning then had to do a jump, run through a tunnel, over the ramp, and then two more jumps.

"For some reason, I wouldn't do the tunnel. I did it on my first lesson, but it didn't matter what was thrown inside the tunnel for me to chase, I would still come out the same way that I went in. This caused lots of laughter", said Eddie Lightning.

The trainers have Jack Russells and know exactly how temperamental they can be, so when Eddie Lightning's mummy kept apologising for his wrong doings, the trainers kept forgiving him.

Little did they know, there would be lots of forgiving to be done over the next few weeks!

"On one of my other turns, I did everything except the tunnel again. Because mummy was still in full flow running, when I stopped suddenly, she tripped up over a clump of grass and went for a tumble. She was ok, apart from a grazed arm", explained a giggly Eddie Lightning.

"Of course, I got the blame, but I can't help it if mummy has two left feet. We won't be heading to Crufts anytime soon or later. However, this agility game is pawsome fun", Eddie laughed.

"After all that excitement, we had some timeout to let another doggy have a go, whilst mummy recovered from her ordeal", said Eddie Lightning, chuckling under his breath.

By the time every other doggy had been around the course, it was the end of the lesson. All the doggies went home tired out and ready for their bed, including Eddie Lightning.

LESSON 3 SHENANIGANS

Eddie Lightning couldn't wait to get back to agility for another week. He saw his friends Skye and Bobby again. They sat patiently, waiting for the lesson to start, like good doggies.

He had other ideas and went wandering off to find treats and to get fuss from people. "Hey there, I am Eddie Lightning, pleased to see you", he would say to everypawdy, as he toddled past them, dragging his mummy along with him.

Eddie Lightning suddenly saw his trainers arrive, so he quickly ran up to them to get his weekly fuss, with his mummy in tow.

His mummy would say "Eddie Lightning, there's not just you here. Give all the other doggies a chance for some fuss".

The trainers would laugh and fuss him regardless. He had that super power 'charm' about him.

Eddie Lightning's mummy laid out his water bowl and got his treats out of the bag, ready to start the lesson, like she did every week.

Every week, he insisted on nudging her to get a treat, each time it wasn't his turn to perform. Sometimes he would succeed, but more often than not he didn't.

His mummy had to keep reminding him that "the treats are for when you have done something good on your turn".

If Skye or Bobby had any treats, Eddie Lightning would try and fuss around their mummies to see if he could get one. Sometimes he was successful and other times he wasn't. When unsuccessful, he would witter to his own mummy for a treat again, until she gave in!

An observer would think Eddie Lightning never got fed. Food is on his mind all of the time and he would never turn it down, unless it was something he didn't like, such as carrots!

"I got bored of waiting to start the lesson, so I decided to go under the table and drink from Bobby's and Skye's water bowls, instead of my own", admitted Eddie Lightning.

Bobby and Skye were so kind that they didn't mind sharing their water with Eddie Lightning.

Once the lesson was underway, the doggies in the class were taught how to use the A -frame.

"Wowza that is a big mean piece of equipment and very high" Eddie Lightning said very loudly. After the shock of being told he had to climb the A-frame, Eddie Lightning was actually pawsome at it, which was surprising.

He said to the trainers "I must have charged up my 'good boy' super powers tonight, BOL". The trainers had to agree with him, but would that last for the rest of the lesson, they wondered!

Eddie Lightning did have a couple of incidents during this lesson, however. He was sick about 30 minutes in and his mummy knew instantly what had caused this to happen.

"I am a devil for eating grass on my walks, but it's better out rather than in, so they say! I do feel pawsome now", said Eddie Lightning, in a guilty tone of voice. His mummy proceeded to clear up the mess, before he could have his turn around the course.

The trainers thought it would be best for Eddie Lightning to miss a turn, so that his tummy could settle down again. His mummy agreed and she did her best to keep him quiet and still, which is no mean feat when you have a bouncy, energetic superhero doggy.

Eddie Lightning and his mummy watched Skye and Bobby taking it in turns to go around the course, like well behaved doggies, with no distractions from him!

The second incident of the evening was on the A-frame.

"I was too busy watching the delicious treat in mummy's hand, that I got too close to the edge and fell off".

"I wasn't hurt, thankfully. My 'brave boy' super powers kicked in and I just stood up, got back on the A-frame and continued where I left off, until the end of the lesson", laughed Eddie Lightning.

"Mummy and the trainers were very proud of me. All in all, this was one of my better lessons, BOL", said Eddie Lightning.

"Mummy and I are very clumsy, one way or another. If it isn't mummy tripping up, it's me falling off things. Oh well, we sure give everypawdy something to laugh about each week! Seven more sleeps and I will be back again in full force", he said joyfully.

LESSON 4 MISCHIEF

Wowza, wowza, oh my doglets (OMD), bark out loud (BOL), this lesson was the most eventful lesson so far for Eddie Lightning and his friends. It was full of mischief, stubbornness and so much fun, BOL. Talk about 'Dogs Behaving Badly', that is an understatement.

The trainers must have felt like packing up and sending us all home and nopawdy would have blamed them.

Lots of names spring to mind to describe the behaviour of Eddie Lightning and his friends that evening. 'Three Amigos', 'The Three PITAs', 'Three Little Monkeys', 'The Stubborn Trio', 'Can't Do, Won't Do Gang' and the list goes on...

Eddie already has plenty of names he goes by... 'Lightning', 'E.L.', 'Eddie L', 'Trouble', 'Evil Genius'!

Eddie Lightning started his lesson as he always did and managed to find a treat or two lurking in the long grass. He would grab it before any other doggy smelt it.

He got his usual fuss from everypawdy and left pMail around the field to mark his territory.

He snoopervised his mummy getting his water, treats and ball out of the bag, in the hope of getting some treats before the lesson began.

This lesson was going to be eventful as the class had to go over a jump, then a steep A-frame and then another jump. Eddie Lightning, Skye and Bobby were the only ones in the class this time, so they got more turns at everything. This was pawsome as they needed more turns, so that they could pawfect their skills, in between the antics that were definitely on the cards.

As you can imagine, Eddie Lightning would again be the instigator of the antics as usual!

Eddie Lightning played 'silly devils' for most of the lesson and kept running off back to Skye and Bobby, instead of finishing the course and his mummy had to keep chasing him to get him back.

"Each time it was my turn, I would do half of the course and then run back to Skye and Bobby, who were sat patiently waiting their turn".

"It wasn't like they were calling me over. I just get distracted very easily", said Eddie Lightning, in a mischievous tone of voice.

Eddie Lightning's mummy was very tired after chasing after him, time and time again. She had to keep the lead in her hand, so that she could put him on it to walk him back to the beginning of the course.

Eddie Lightning got to believing it was a new game. He runs off, his mummy chases him and brings him back, then he runs off again. Even treats didn't stop him. He certainly had his 'mischievous' super powers turned on full that night.

Skye wouldn't do the A-frame in the beginning, as it was too steep for her. By the end of the lesson, we all had individual ideas on what we would do and when, apart from Bobby, who did everything right first time BOL.

Skye decided instead of going on the A-frame, she would go over the jumps and through the tunnel. She was fandabedozie at doing that, which gave her lots of confidence.

She completed a number of rounds over the jumps and through the tunnels, without a care in the world. It was like the A-frame was invisible to her, as she ran stubbornly past it, on a mission to avoid it.

She was on a roll and did great doing what she wanted to do!

Little did she know what was coming next!

Syke was eventually made to go on the A-frame before the end of the lesson, with help both sides at first. She did it again with help on one side and then, for a third time, all by herself. She managed to repeat this by herself a few more times. This was pawtastic and Skye was feeling very happy. She was beaming from ear to ear!

Everpawdy was so proud of Skye for not giving up. The hoomans all started clapping and all the doggies barked out loud (BOL).

Bobby did pawsome for the whole lesson. He attempted everything he was asked to do and did it right first time. Everypawdy clapped and barked out loud (BOL) for Bobby. Bobby was very excited that he did everything right and he had a well-earned treat!

Maybe the new names for Lightning and his friends should be re-assessed, as they had all managed to do some good this time, apart from Eddie Lightning himself, of course!

After numerous times of Eddie Lightning running off back to his friends, half way around the course, his mummy decided to do the course the opposite way around. That way he couldn't see his friends and it would help him focus more.

This was pawfect, as he managed to do the course three times without getting distracted. What an achievement for such a mischievous doggy. Everypawdy clapped and cheered as he finished his turn.

He ran off back to his friends with his tail wagging with excitement.

His mummy was thinking "He can behave when he wants to, the little hooligan!"

Eddie Lightning and his friends were the entertainment for the evening and had everypawdy crying with laughter, yet again. They couldn't wait to entertain again next week.

LESSON 5 FUN

Again, at agility this time, Eddie Lightning was being a bit temperamental (wowza that's a big word for a little doggy!).

"I should know by now, if I do it right, I get treats at the end. To say I'm a superhero, I'm a bit lacking in the 'common sense' department when it comes to joining up the treat dots BOL", admitted Eddie Lightning.

"There were only three of us again for this lesson; me, Skye and Bobby."

"We had more turns, which resulted in us all getting tired quicker. I was definitely in Eddie Lightning mode, even if I did it wrong, I still ran like the speed of light.

I met a new friend called Lola. She was an 18-month-old pug. We shared our water bowls and treats with each other. Lola had been doing agility for longer and was very good at it. She was in the advanced class."

During this lesson, Eddie Lightning had to jump over three jumps; one at an angle, so mummy had to turn the correct way to get me over it; through a tunnel and over a 4th jump. This was pawsome fun and Eddie Lightning certainly made his mummy work hard.

He was super charged with energy that evening and ran like a 'bolt of lightning' around the course.

His mummy was struggling to catch her breath, as he was running so fast. He went round the course a few times, some jumps he missed, but on the whole he behaved and did what he was asked to do.

"I did stop in my tracks a couple of times, as I smelt a treat and was compelled to get it, before any other doggy beat me to it", exclaimed Eddie Lightning.

One occasion, straight after one of Eddie Lightning's turns, he bolted over to the advanced class to say hello to the doggies. He didn't care that he was running into the path of a doggy doing their turn around the course BOL.

His mummy chased after him to get him on his lead. It was like a comedy sketch chasing him across the field. His mummy was so embarrassed. "It was a good job the lesson was coming to an end, as I seemed to have more energy then, than I had at the beginning", said Eddie Lightning.

All of the other doggies had to stop what they were doing until Eddie Lightning's mummy had got him back on the lead. That task took quite a while, as his mummy was exhausted, but Eddie Lightning was still full of super power 'beans'.

Once he was back with his own class, the advanced class could carry on, minus the intruder, until the end of the lesson.

Eddie Lightning prefers to ask for forgiveness afterwards rather than permission at the start! That's more fun!

LESSON 6 CHAOS

When Eddie Lightning and his mummy arrived at agility this time, they were the only ones there, so Eddie Lightning got a one-to-one lesson, with the trainers. Or so he thought!

Eddie Lightning was doing great, but then his friend Bobby arrived later, so things took a turn for the worst.

They took it in turns to do the course, however all Eddie Lightning had on his mind was antics, antics and more antics.

They had to jump over a jump, through the tunnel, over another jump, turn left, over two jumps, turn right and over two more jumps.

"Mummy says I was a bad boy when Bobby arrived. I was doing fine, but then I would only do the first jump, tunnel and second jump before running to Bobby", Eddie Lightning giggled. One of the trainers had to stand in his escape route to guide him back to the course.

"I got to the 5th hurdle and then ran off course to explore smells that smelt like delicious treats. By the end, I decided I wasn't even going to go in the tunnel", he admitted.

The trainers thought that Eddie Lightning was behaving like this because there were only two of them, and only him at the beginning, so he was getting tired more quickly, as he was having more turns around the course than normal.

Mummy said "It was payback to me for leaving him on his own all day when I went to work". I replied "You are probably right!"

Thankfully for Eddie Lightning, Bobby was being quite a bit temperamental too. He kept jumping at his mummy for his treat and missing out jumps. The trainers must have thought they had both lost the plot during this lesson. "Better luck next week", was said by all.

LESSON 7 FINALE

As with other lessons, Eddie Lightning continued to entertain with his silly mischievous antics.

He was the only one at the lesson at the beginning again. The other doggies arrived later.

He wouldn't listen to his mummy at the start of each turn. His mummy was asking him to stay and wait, but he wanted to get on with things, as his super powers were charged and ready to go! One of the trainers had to hold him back like they used to in the first couple of lessons, until he decided to wait by himself. This took a number of goes to be pawfect.

He was certainly determined with his 'entertaining' super powers to make everypawdy laugh again and he succeeded, even without his doggy friends as a distraction at the beginning! "Who needs an audience to misbehave?", said Eddie Lightning cheekily.

As Eddie Lightning ran around the course, he smelt something nice. He would run off to sniff the smell, before re-joining, in his own good time. Everypawdy else had to wait around for him to return BOL.

This lesson was the last one before the Christmas break, so Eddie Lightning wanted to go out in style, to show just how much he had really learnt in the seven lessons he had completed.

His super power 'lightning speeds' were rocketing.
The only thing that held him back was his exhausted mummy! By the end of the lesson, he was performing to pawfection and there was no stopping him!

Eddie Lightning and his mummy packed up their things and headed back home for a fandabedozie Christmas and a very long sleep.

THE END

ACKNOWLEDGEMENTS

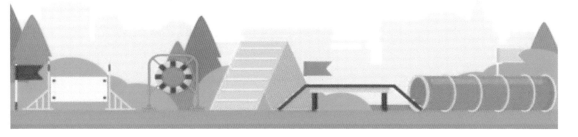

pixabay.com
istockphoto.com
book creator.com
freesvg.org

ABOUT THE AUTHOR

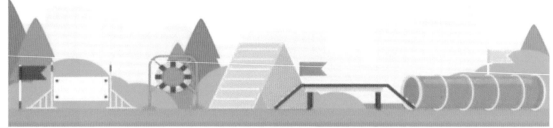

Jayne Norman is a fictional author, who writes short stories about her Jack Russell Terrier called Eddie. He is a mischievous and fun-loving dog, who can run like the speed of light (hence the name Eddie Lightning).

'The Adventures of Eddie Lightning' Book Series gives an insight into Eddie's day to day life, the adventures he goes on and the mischief along the way.

THE ADVENTURES OF EDDIE LIGHTNING PUBLISHED BOOKS:

Book 1

Six Sides to Eddie Lightning &
Seven Days in the Life of a Superhero

Book 2

Shenanigans in the Snow

Book 3

Antics at Agility

THE ADVENTURES OF EDDIE LIGHTNING BOOKS TO LOOK OUT FOR:

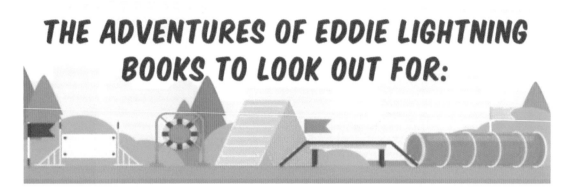

Book 4
Laughter in the Lake

Book 5
Bath Time Bonanza

Book 6
Venturesome Vacations

Printed in Great Britain
by Amazon